Something, someday

words by
Amanda Gorman

pictures by
Christian Robinson

VIKING

You are told
That this is not a problem.
But you're sure
There's something wrong.

You are told that this cannot be fixed.
But you know that you can help.

You are told that this is too big for you.
But you've seen the tiniest things
Make a huge difference.

You're told that this won't work,
But how will you know
If you never try?

You're told to sit and wait,
But you know people
Have already waited
Too long.

You're told
That what's going on
Is very, very sad.
But you're not just sad.

You're scared.
And confused.
You're angry.

And maybe,
Just maybe,
A little hopeful.

You're told not to hope.

But you keep hoping anyway.

Sometimes you feel like you're all alone.

But someday, somewhere,
You find a friend.
Someone who will hope with you,
Who believes in your dream.
Someone who will fight with you.

You make a promise
To each other.

You say:
"There is a problem,
But it's our problem together,
So we can fix it together.

This problem is big,
But together,

We are bigger."

You make another friend
And tell them:
"It's okay to be sad."

And they tell you:
"Sometimes we'll lose.
But that's all right,
We'll try again."

And so you do.
Together, working.
Together, beginning,
Over and over
And over and over.

Until you're no longer beginning.

You're winning.

Suddenly, there's something
You're sure is right.
Something you know
You helped fix.
Something small that changed—
Something big.

Something that worked.
Something that makes you feel
Hopeful, happy, and loved.

Something that is not a dream,
But the day you live in.

Something that makes you smile
As you tell someone else.

For my agent, Steve Malk—
I'm so grateful to reach something, someday, with you. —A. G.

For Thầy —C. R.

VIKING
An imprint of Penguin Random House LLC, New York

First published in the United States of America by Viking, an imprint of Penguin Random House LLC, 2023

Text copyright © 2023 by Amanda Gorman
Art copyright © 2023 by Christian Robinson

Visit us online at PenguinRandomHouse.com.

Library of Congress Cataloging-in-Publication Data is available.

Printed in the United States of America

ISBN 9780593203255

1   3   5   7   9   10   8   6   4   2

WOR

Design by Christian Robinson and Jim Hoover. Text set in Marion Regular.
The art for this book was created with paint, collage, and digital manipulation.